To every child who has ever discovered
the magic of science

All rights reserved. Published in the United States by Crown Books for Young Readers,
an imprint of Random House Children's Books, a division of Penguin Random House LLC, New York.

Crown and the colophon are registered trademarks of Penguin Random House LLC.

Visit us on the Web! rhcbooks.com

Educators and librarians, for a variety of teaching tools, visit us at RHTeachersLibrarians.com

Library of Congress Cataloging-in-Publication Data is available upon request.
ISBN 978-0-525-58139-0 (trade) — ISBN 978-0-525-58140-6 (lib. bdg.) — ISBN 978-0-525-58141-3 (ebook)

The artwork for this book was rendered digitally after wishing on a star,
planting it in soil, and giving it plenty of sunlight.

Book design by Nicole de las Heras

MANUFACTURED IN CHINA
10 9 8 7 6 5 4 3 2 1
First Edition

FAIRY SCIENCE

Ashley Spires

Crown Books for Young Readers
New York

Esther does not believe in magic.

This is unusual because Esther is a
fairy, and fairies are all about magic.

They use magic wands, and they mix magic potions.
Some fairies even make magical fairy dust.

Esther is pretty sure that's just dandruff.

She is the only fairy in Pixieville who believes in science.

ALBERT'S OBSERVATORY NEST

Esther prefers facts, data, and hard evidence to wishing on stars.

Unfortunately, the only thing they teach in fairy school is magic. Class is very frustrating for Esther.

And for Ms. Pelly Petal.

Esther can't help observing the world differently from everyone else. Where other fairies see a path to hidden gold, Esther sees light and water colliding.

Follow the rainbow!

The water helps us see all the colors that are hidden in the sunlight! That's dispersion.

Where they see a dangerous omen, she sees condensation.

Where they see faces of the spirits, she sees erosion.

Esther can't wait to teach the scientific method to her fairymates.

She shows them the periodic table.

PING

THEY JUST DON'T GET IT!

That was definitely gravity.

And there is definitely something wrong with this tree.

It's wilting.

The fairies do their best to help.
They cast spells.

They make magic talismans.

They even do a mystical moonlight dance.

But nothing works. The tree keeps on wilting.
Esther asks a question.

Why is the tree wilting?

She does some research.

WHAT I KNOW ABOUT TREES
1) They have leaves.
2) They have roots.
3) They are pretty.
4) They grow out of dirt.

She makes a hypothesis.

She tries some experiments.

She studies her results.

At last, Esther draws a conclusion!

Now she waits for the sun to do its work.

It took a while, but the tree is looking positively perky.

She did it! Esther has proven the power of science!

Ms. Pelly Petal did it! Magic saved the tree!

At least she *thought* she did.

She might not have changed the other fairies' minds . . .

But Esther has inspired some questions.

And that's where every good scientist starts.

ESTHER'S SUN-BEAN EXPERIMENT

You don't have to be a fairy to do a science experiment! Why not grow your own seedlings at home? You'll need these things:

Experiment Checklist:

Dried Lima Beans

A Zip-Seal Sandwich Bag

A Paper Towel

Tape

Your beans will grow extra fast if you soak them overnight!

First, fold your paper towel in half and then in half again so it makes a square.

Next, wet the paper towel. It should be damp but not dripping wet.

Place the paper towel in the zip-seal bag along with three or four lima beans.

Plants need lots of room to grow, so don't add too many beans!

Finally, seal up the bag and tape it to a well-lit window. Just like our tree, these plants need sun to grow!

Ta-da!

Once your experiment is set, make a hypothesis about how long you think it will take the seedlings to grow.

This is called germination.

Study your results every day to see how your seeds change and make conclusions about what you see!

That's the scientific method!